BABAR
and the Wully-Wully

BABAR

Laurent de Brunhoff

and the Wully-Wully

Harry N. Abrams, Inc., Publishers

In the country of the elephants, Pom, Flora, and Alexander, the children of King Babar and Queen Celeste, took a stroll. Suddenly they found themselves face-to-face with a strange little animal.

"What is that?" whispered Flora.

"A Wully-Wully," answered Pom, who always knew everything.

"A what?"

"A Wully-Wully. An animal that is seldom seen."

"Let's take him home with us," said Alexander.

Flora cuddled the little animal in her arms.

"M-m-m . . ." she hummed. "His fur is so soft."

In the gardens at Celesteville, the city of the elephants, Babar said, "Yes, this is certainly a Wully-Wully. He is very gentle looking and quite lovable."

The Old Lady, a close friend of the Babar family, smiled fondly

at the small creature, but Zephir the monkey acted reserved. Babar's young cousin Arthur quickly took some photos.

"My goodness!" exclaimed old General Cornelius. "What an event! I haven't seen a Wully-Wully in almost ten years."

The Wully-Wully had a
very good time in
Babar's house.
The toys of Pom,
Flora, and Alexander
fascinated him,
especially the electric
train. He watched it
go around him hour
after hour.

Wully-Wully also liked to play hide and seek. He would steal
off quietly and hide in all sorts of places—under a chair . . .
behind the drapes. . . . He was difficult to find because he made
no more noise than a feather.

The Wully-Wully ate with the rest of the family, but instead of sitting down with them he preferred to hang upside down by his tail. He also slept in that position, like a bat.

Wully-Wully was really very happy in Celesteville. Every day he discovered astonishing new things. Arthur taught him to blow into a saxophone. Wully-Wully made some loud squawks and everybody burst out laughing.

But Wully-Wully liked the country even better, so the children took him on a picnic. While they unpacked the food, Rataxes the rhinoceros was spying on them.

"A Wully-Wully!" he said. "If I can snatch him away, he'll be mine!"

The little pet suspected nothing, and neither did the children.

Suddenly Rataxes jumped out from behind the bush, shoved the little elephants out of the way, and seized the Wully-Wully, who let out a piercing cry. But what could he do against a huge rhinoceros?

Rataxes jumped into his car with the Wully-Wully and drove off, laughing loudly. Arthur and the others tried to chase after him, but the thief got away. They were all in despair. They thought they had lost their little Wully-Wully forever.

They rushed back to the garden to find Zephir.
   "You must help us," said Pom.

After he had heard the whole story, the monkey said, "Arthur, let's go on a search."

The two scouts crept up to the city of the rhinos. Zephir looked through his binoculars.

He saw the Wully-Wully tied by a leash. Rataxes didn't let the little creature loose for an instant.

To get closer to the city without being seen, Arthur put on one of his disguises.

Dressed like a camel, he walked behind the bushes. Zephir looked like someone out for a ride.

They saw that Wully-Wully looked very unhappy. "How can we save him?" Arthur asked.

"Just you wait, Rataxes!" threatened Zephir. "I am going to think up a trick to get into your city."

Later that day a strange hat merchant arrived in the city of the rhinos. Everybody rushed to the city square, for the rhinos all adore hats.

Suddenly Rataxes cried, "Arthur, you rascal! I recognize you! A hat merchant indeed! You want to take back the Wully-Wully, don't you? But you can't fool me. It's off to prison for you!"

In the garden at Celesteville, Pom, Flora, and Alexander were waiting. Zephir had promised to be back with the Wully-Wully in two hours.

Alexander climbed to the top of a tree to watch for their arrival, but no one came. The road was empty.

The hours passed. Flora cried. Pom comforted her. "Come," he said. "Let's find Papa."

That evening everybody was very worried. Cornelius played cards, but he could not hide his concern. "You never know what that Rataxes will do," he said. The Old Lady agreed.

Babar tried to reassure them. "You just wait," he said. "Arthur and Zephir will be successful. Don't worry."

The children went to bed. But Flora could not sleep. She was too sad.

All this time Arthur had been shut up in a tiny, dark cell. Fortunately, Rataxes had not caught Zephir. The clever monkey had managed to get away and was hiding nearby.

As soon as darkness fell, he ran up to the prison and shouted, "Arthur! I am going to save you! Have courage!" The guards, outraged by this impudence, chased after him.

It was easy for Zephir to lead the clumsy rhinos away from the prison. They puffed along behind him, shouting, "Beware, you monkey! We'll fix you!"

Suddenly, without knowing how it happened, the guards lost all trace of Zephir.

Where had he gone?

They couldn't believe it!

After leading the guards astray, Zephir quickly went back to the prison. He got the door open. Arthur was free!

"Wait for me in the woods, Arthur," said Zephir. "I am going to set the Wully-Wully free before anyone can give the alarm."

Quietly as a cat, Zephir crept inside Rataxes's palace. Arthur watched him vanish right under the noses of the sleeping guards.

Zephir found
Rataxes's bedroom
without any trouble. The big
rhinoceros was sleeping like a log
under his heavy quilt. His stomach went up
and down when he breathed. Wully-Wully
wagged his tail, for he recognized the
little monkey.

"Shh!" Zephir warned. He took
the Wully-Wully in his arms and
stole away as silently as he
had come in.

Zephir and the Wully-Wully found Arthur and, without losing a second, all three of them left the city. Soon they were far away, and Zephir began to chuckle.

"Rataxes is going to make a funny face when he wakes up!"

Very early in the morning Babar and Celeste heard shouts under their windows. Everybody rushed out to greet the returning heroes, who were very proud of their escapade.

"Good gracious!" exclaimed the Old Lady. "What a relief! I didn't sleep all night." And Flora hugged her Wully-Wully.

The news spread very fast through Celesteville. The elephants gathered to congratulate Arthur and Zephir. They carried them in triumph through the streets.

"Bravo, Arthur! Bravo, Zephir!" they shouted. "You have outwitted Rataxes! Bravo! Long live the Wully-Wully."

Pom, Flora, and Alexander went off by themselves, taking the Wully-Wully with them.

"Tell us all about it, Wully," said Flora as she scratched her pet's back. Wully-Wully twitched his whiskers and smiled.

But suddenly they heard a frightful rumbling like an earthquake!

It was Rataxes and his rhinos, sweeping through Celesteville
like a hurricane. The elephants were so stunned by this terrible

charge that they could not even resist. The rhinos disappeared
in a cloud of dust, carrying Wully-Wully away with them.

Babar immediately called all the elephants together. Cornelius and his soldiers stood beside him. The elephants were furious. They shouted, "Down with Rataxes! Let's go after the thieves! We want to fight!"

Babar did not want to go to war, but what could he do?

Little Flora was worried.
She started thinking:
   "If there is a war with
the rhinos, what will happen
to Wully? He could be killed.
And if he dies, there will be
no more Wully-Wully."

Flora decided that she would go to find Rataxes. "I will explain all this to him," she thought.
   Without saying anything to anyone, she left Celesteville. As fast as she could go, she ran straight to the city of the rhinos.

When the guards brought the spunky little elephant to Rataxes, the fierce old rhinoceros scowled and said, "What have you come here for? Aren't you afraid?"

"Why should I be?" asked Flora.

"Well, you know that Arthur and Zephir played a trick on me!" said Rataxes.

Flora did not answer. Instead she asked, "Why do you keep poor Wully-Wully in a cage? And why did you steal him? He is not yours."

"He is not yours either!" grumbled Rataxes.

"You are right. He isn't really mine. But I am the one who found him and I never tied him up. I didn't put him in a cage either, yet he stayed with me."

Perplexed, Rataxes scratched his ear. "If I let him out of the cage, he will run away."

"Perhaps," said Flora. "But he will come back when he wants to."

Still troubled, Rataxes opened the cage.

"Little girl," he said, "I think you are trying to twist me around your little trunk."

Now the Wully-Wully can go where he wishes. Each day he usually stops to see Flora and the elephants, but he also visits in the city of the rhinos. When Wully-Wully is at Celesteville, Rataxes is likely to be there, too, helping Flora make a rope swing for the little pet.

Babar watches them and thinks, "It's really amazing. Our little Flora has completely tamed the great, rough Rataxes!"

DESIGNER, ABRAMS EDITION: Darilyn Lowe Carnes

The artwork for each picture is prepared using watercolor on paper.
This text is set in 16-point Comic Sans.

Library of Congress Cataloging-in-Publication Data

Brunhoff, Laurent de.
    [Babar et le Wouly-Wouly. English]
    Babar and the Wully-Wully / Laurent de Brunhoff.
       p. cm.
    Summary: The children of Babar the elephant want to keep the
Wully-Wully they find as a pet, but a rhinoceros steals him.
    ISBN 0-8109-4397-2
    [1. Elephants—Fiction. 2. Pets—Fiction. 3. Rhinoceroses—Fiction.]
I. Title.
  PZ7.B82843 Baak 2001
  [E]—dc21   00-051083

PRINTED AND BOUND IN BELGIUM

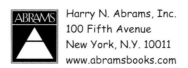
Harry N. Abrams, Inc.
100 Fifth Avenue
New York, N.Y. 10011
www.abramsbooks.com